LIGHTS, CAMERA, *and* ACTION

3 Steps to Being
the Star of Your Own Life

LYZANDER VEREEN

ISBN: 978-1-7347102-0-5 (Paperback)
ISBN: 978-1-7347102-1-2 (Ebook)

This book is not intended as a substitute for psychological or medical advice. The methods described in this book are the author's personal thoughts. Any use of this information is at your own discretion.

Book design by PixelStudio.
Edited by Erica James of Masterpieces Writing and Editing LLC.

Printed by The Aquarian Projects LLC, in the United States of America.

First printing edition 2020.

The Aquarian Projects LLC
www.aquarianmotiv8.com

Table of Contents

Introduction

"What can I say about life . . . sometimes it sucks!" This is something I would have said as the old me as little as a year ago, maybe even a couple of months ago. However, now, I would say that life is just a bunch of opportunities from which we learn and grow. Of course, life is going to have the ups and downs and twists and turns that every roller coaster ride has. It may even take you for a loop, taking you back to a place from where you thought you had moved on. Nevertheless, it is up to us to be brave and ride the ride, to make every twist and turn count as a step to enjoyment. Or we can give in to our fears and miss all of the excitement along what could be an amazing ride.

For a long time, I sat in the funk of believing that life sometimes sucked. During those times, many factors influenced my way of thinking. In short, I believed so many obstacles blocked my path to happiness. My career was not in a place I was proud of. My education level was not one that reflected my intelligence or capability, and it held me back from achieving the career I wanted. Without the career I desired, I was not securing enough income to sustain even a complacent life. I was always running and worrying about the money I would never have. As a result, I was a failure to my altruistic nature, not giving my time and effort or much thought to giving to others. I was not fulfilling my duties as a father: being a provider and source of inspiration for my family, showing my kids how to be better. Most of all, I was not being a husband to my wife, providing for her needs as a husband should, which led to a difficult separation that ultimately ended in divorce. Yes, things in life sometimes suck . . . and the more one thing sucks, the more other shit keeps sucking. And as shit does, it keeps piling and piling and piling until the suckiness becomes overwhelming. Instead of this or that sucking, it just becomes, "It's really life that sucks."

I believed life sucked so bad that I became scared to live it. I decided to hide as much as I could and slumped into a depression. The hurt became so bad that even suicide became a real life thought for me. I was so influenced by the negative things around me that I became intoxicated with the pain, hurt, guilt, regret, sadness, self-loathing, self-pity, and eventually the denial that I, MYSELF, had anything to do with MYSELF and the negative state I was in.

Before I state the moment that changed my perspective of MY life, I want everyone reading this book to realize that this is not the way it is for everyone. This is my personal account, and as we are all different, our souls, the universe and God speak to us in different ways. Sometimes we see it and sometimes we don't, and for some it doesn't happen. For some it is an unconscious tangent, while for others it is a conscious action. I want to be an inspiration, but I realize I cannot be that to all. The following dream was my moment. And with all wishes, I hope it inspires yours to begin or continue.

My Dream

Out of blur and a sense of journey and adventure, I awoke into a vision. Even though I had not actually taken the journey physically, I could sense that I had just emerged from a series of events that involved exerting quite a bit of energy, sweat, and acquiring layers of muck that stuck to my overgrown five-day shadow of a beard.

From this point, I began to envision what lied ahead of me. Behind a shade of a couple of overgrown leaves was a clearing. A clearing that sparkled with something there, not quite decipherable with the leaves in the way, so I pushed them aside. In the clearing there was a tree, a big tree. There was nothing special about the tree, but you could tell it was important, like it was me. To the sides of the tree emerged two very different objects.

On one side, there was a lovely unicorn with a black coat so shiny that you could see your reflection, yet soft, fluffy and made of pillowing clouds that brewed thunderstorms under each lock of hair. Her mane was dazzling, silken and elegant, yet refined and very well cared for. Although lovely it looked, it was chained and therefore ill-tempered. Her eyes that dazzled and illuminated like fiery diamonds drew me in close to look at her, to touch her and to feel her, but she still fought me to be the wild animal she was meant to be. With each caress of her mane, she gave me a gentle neigh for pleasure and comfort, but still bucked and reared to let me know she could never be mine . . . for she is hers. And even as I pleaded with the unicorn that I would not hold her captive, but allow her to grow wings, give her the strength she has and the strength only she could imagine, it calmed the unicorn for a while but not entirely.

On the other side was a pot of gold with a rainbow extending from its golden luster and glaze. A pot of gold . . . just like a leprechaun's pot of gold. The rainbow extending from it inlaid with every color imaginable, all with its own unique jewel-like luster, like a beautiful bridge made of glittering and glassy light. At some points along the rainbow were different lands, none that we know of, all imaginary lands. In between the imaginary lands, inlaid in the rainbow, emerged images of faces of people who the rainbow would encounter, images of places the rainbow could go, and images of things the rainbow could do. A pot of gold that opened up the world!

The intent was evident and a choice was to be made between each. However, the choice is not without signs and deeper choices. For as long as I held the unicorn in my captivity, the unicorn would never change who the unicorn was. And no matter how many chains I took off of the unicorn, it would always be my captive. As for the pot of gold, the choice was freedom and a chance to live out my dreams of anything. The opportunity is there, and the road is laid out. My choice. My choice says the tree . . . that I still believe is me!

So I made a choice!

Having a dream like that one would inspire anyone to reevaluate their life. It was then that I realized that life does not suck, not sometimes, not ever. It was MYSELF that sucked and that had to stop! I generally was okay, and everything around me was not killing me, but my thoughts and perspective on life sucked. In turn, even the things that were intended to be a lesson or good for me sucked, too. Therefore, it took learning that life is meant to be lived with only the constraints that we place on ourselves. What a lesson to learn and what a way to learn it!

The interpretation of the dream is that we are not simply rooted in choices but more so in the perspective in which we hold those choices. Life itself is the web of choices that we have made in many different circumstances, and how we perceived life in those moments determined how we made our choice. Though many of us are able to reach this realization, most of us fail to realize the very notion that my dream highlighted: many choices are not only decided by our perspectives but also derived from our perspectives. That is correct. Many of the choices we face result from the perspectives we carry in life. Simply put, someone with a positive outlook on life will have many more perceived opportunities than someone who has a negative outlook on life. For example, let's say you score the very last seat on the subway before anyone has to stand. The next stop then comes and a few people get on the train. Now there is a person who asks to sit in your seat. You get up and give them the seat, but here is where perspective makes a difference. For the burdened you, this is an opportunity to sit down taken away from you. However, for the positive you, this is an opportunity to lose some calories by standing because it will benefit you in the long run. This is how the train of thought can continue and so will the choices that must be made. Because the burdened you had to stand, you have the choice either to whine about your calf muscle being sore or to walk it out with your thoughts on the day ahead. Choosing to dwell on the soreness, you decide not to be productive at work and get that report done all because you chose to give up your seat. And vice versa: the positive you feels more energized from the standing then chooses to walk to work and to stroll through the park, where you meet your celebrity crush. Now you have the opportunity to choose to give your crush your phone number or to remain faithful to your boyfriend/girlfriend. As for me, it is a no-brainer: my celebrity crush is definitely getting these digits!

As demonstrated in the previous example,

perspectives can promote stagnation and even declination, as well as generate burdensome tasks and habits that negatively affect our lives. Or they can promote learning and experience, where there is not an option of failure but one to learn how to try things differently to succeed. This is how the perspectives that we carry can hinder or help guide us to better choices in life.

The process of change can be hard for some people, as it was for myself. When we are unable to change things that are harmful to our progress, we tend to spiral into a life that is not fruitful or satisfying, as was my life. It also seemed as if no matter how much I tried to change things, they did not budge. Back then, I could spend days reviewing the list of things that were going horribly wrong for me. I lost some jobs, some self-confidence, and my source of income, which led to me feeling unworthy. This feeling began to ooze into my marriage and relationships with family and friends. Whatever aspect of my life you named, something was going wrong with it. There seemed to be no end in sight all because I was "stuck"!

"Being stuck" was my go-to excuse for everything that I would start and never finish, for all of the opportunities I missed out on, especially those that I never even attempted. I referred to all of my failures and weaknesses as being stuck. Many of us may call it different things, such as being broke, having no job or a bad job, having no luck in love or having a bad love life, or just not being in a place to grow. But whatever you call it, it is your idea of being stuck.

So if all of this can describe being stuck, then what is it really? From my clients, and even my own self-observation, I have found that being stuck is knowing that we are capable of doing differently to become better. And contrary to knowing this, for some reason we keep ourselves in a state of a repetitively poor mindset that hinders growth in particular areas but has an overall impact on our whole being and life. It is a state of confusion about who we are and what we want out of life. It is continual condescension and criticism of ourselves that does not allow for the better. When we perceive all of our negatives outweighing our positives, this is being stuck. Being stuck is a state-of-mind that has roots somewhere deep in our psyche, and this governs our habits and actions. When stuck, we are in a pattern of non-growth and progress for ourselves. It may sound confusing, but to be stuck you do have to know and envision that things could be better, or that you could be better off.

One of my own personal quips that keeps me stuck in a rut is my inability to see my own value and worth, especially when conceptualizing businesses. In general, I know I have all of these wonderful ideas, and all I need to do is sell myself to sell them. However, one question has always loomed over me, often keeping me from being a successful entrepreneur: "I have nothing but an idea, so why would anyone listen to me?"

For instance, about fifteen years ago, I had a business idea to open an indoor playground in Miami. For this particular business, I did everything that was needed to start a business. I got the licenses I needed. I completed all of the legal structure. I drafted a highly comprehensive business plan. I did all of the research and gathered quotes for equipment, locations and even insurances I would need. I devised a marketing plan and was already spreading the word that I wanted to open this business. I did all of the necessary grunt work, all of the work I could do on my own, and I was ready to start this business and grow it. Now I just needed some partnership, networking and funding. Before I tell you what happened next, I went through this whole process three more times with three other business ideas: conceptualized, planned and legally organized, the whole works. However, for each idea, the fruition went nowhere because I always reached a point where I needed to open my mouth and ask for help. This mostly happened when I needed to find either partnerships, funding or patronage. All of these motions had one thing in common: I had to talk to people about my ideas, which was fine. But when I had to explain why they should help me, I would be at a loss for words. I never had the gumption to ask anyone directly for the assistance. To mask this flaw, I even had a few crowdfunding campaigns to excuse me for not asking anyone personally. And they all failed, mainly because even there I was too afraid to sell who I really am and what I really could do. For the longest, I would blame others for not helping me, or blame my ideas for being terrible. But the real culprit was ME, being stuck in a mindset of unworthiness. In this state, I continued to fail until I realized I had to change my mindset about myself and my ideas. I had to see them as worthy and valuable.

If there is anyone I aim to help with this book, it is those who are stuck. You are my kindred people. You may have experienced a situation similar to mine and just labeled your excuse as something different, such as no money, no job, a bad love life, introvertedness, reclusiveness, and the list goes on! You are all part of my being stuck family. Welcome to the table! Let's see if we can get a little "unstuck"!

Through the difficulty of being stuck arose a breaking point. I realized that I was stuck and consistently reinforcing that stickiness with my perceptions, communication and habits. It was difficult to accept that I was constantly existing in a negative space, consistently lacking confidence in myself, and habitually placing myself in circumstances that I knew did not provide any growth. However, this led to my shift from the "stuck mindset" to the unstuck mindset. Being unstuck was literally the act of reenvisioning my negatives and focusing on how to make them positive. It involved taking action to remove anything that was not growth-related and to replace them with things that served me. Becoming unstuck involved using my own ability to take control of the general progression of my life.

By seeking out the greatest people to help develop routines and habits, all the while recording my process of development, I was able to keep up with stable progress and make efficient changes. But then I thought, if I was able to do it, then I know YOU can, too. This thought birthed *Lights, Camera, and Action*!

Welcome to *Lights, Camera, and Action*, a book where I describe for you the path of change. And how I, and others, have used the process and benefited from it all. Why is the process of change referred to as Lights, Camera, and Action? We have all heard a version of the phrase, "Life is a stage, and we are all its actors." However, what this phrase does not state is that we are our own production crew as well. Being the production crew gives us the ability to not be mere actors portraying a story, but the creator, director, producer and stars of our lives. This process aims to enhance the most important aspects for progressional change within you, your mindset and your actions. *Lights, Camera, and Action* aims to place your attention on your growth through the process of change. It focuses on the following three main aspects:

- Observation: taking a good, hard look at yourself, shining a light on every aspect of your mindset and actions

- Analyzing: making choices that change the focus of who you are and what you actually can do

- Action: taking the actual steps toward that change that you have envisioned

Throughout each chapter, you will find different tasks and exercises that will help you along your journey. It is important that you are active in these tasks. While I do not expect everyone to complete them all, as each process is different for each person, no progress will occur without trying any tasks. This book is not just for you to read, but for you to participate in. Highlight the information you find important. Write notes in areas you might need to reassess. Track your progress. Think of this book as a TOOL, your tool to becoming "the star of your life". So use it well, use it wisely, and be proud of what you will achieve from it.

If you are still reading this, then I assume you are dedicated to becoming the star of your life. This book is not a quick fix, or an elevator ride to your goals. This book is a stairway, one that will be long and tough. Congratulations on taking this first step. The moment you reach your goals, you will look back and be proud of your progress. Furthermore, you will realize each step is a skill or lesson learned. There is no such thing as failure; even a step back makes it easier to get back up and keep climbing to your goals. Remember, this is not just a motivational or self-help book; it is a workbook to help you actively live. Better yet, it is your screenplay because you are the star of your life.

So, if you are ready, let's jump into the process of your progress and make you the headline star on the stage of your life! Lights, Camera, and Action!

Pre-production

The development of the pre-production process derives from me actually living through this process, going through each step and making them part of my everyday life. Before I begin with the process of Lights, Camera, and Action, let's talk a little about change. To be honest, change is what we fear and rebel against the most. I generally find that people categorize change in two ways. Some people see change as a building block to grow upon and internally nurturing. People who are fluid, invigorated and unstuck find the lessons in change easily and welcome new changes for their growth. They are able to deal with frequent change and handle it all with ease and comfort.

However, for many, it is not a comfortable task at all, the main reason being we are unable to change. Usually, I find that we see change as more than just a variation in routines, places or people. We often see change as a personal attack, as opposed to a means of growth. This is especially true when something external influences this change. But honestly, in full disclosure, I believe that external catalysts are extremely few and far between due to those circumstances being determined by the choices we have made and any other internal change that we have or have not made. The difference in us is that we need change to fix personal defects, which becomes an admittance to our inefficiencies or incapabilities. Because we hold this viewpoint, the process of change becomes a self-defeating task, which enables us to find false contentment in our stuck state. For example, when you say you want to become a world class swimmer and win swimming medals but end up sitting in the house instead, it is not because of a shortage of methods to get there or it being an impossibility. It is usually due to seeing an inefficiency in yourself, thus beginning the self-defeating process.

First, we will state what we want out of life: "I really want to be a world class swimmer." I am willing to bet you were so sure about it that you made a declarative statement. No wishy-washy statement about what you want, but a pretty straight to the point goal. We then start to question the tasks to meet the goal and whether it fits who we are, which is ironic because the whole point of the process is to become someone other than who you are right now. Here is an example: "I know I have to start swimming, which means going to the pool, working out, eating right. So much to do. Plus, I really like McKingDy's burgers. Maybe I'm not a world class swimmer type. And I don't even know how to swim." Next, we tend to become fortune tellers and see our failures beforehand and use them as a reasoning to not do anything now: "If I told anyone that I wanted to be a world class swimmer, they would just laugh at me. Plus, I probably wouldn't even go to all of my swim lessons, or I'm just so goofy that I'd sink, drown, and fail the class anyway." Lastly, we settle for the state that we are currently in, believing that the change is not needed, and therefore never pursue an opportunity to grow externally or internally. We might state: "You know what, I'm cool without being a world class swimmer even though learning how to swim, going to the pool, working out, and eating better would benefit me in all ways."

I know these steps because I experienced them while in a stuck state, not moving forward toward my goals. How do I know these excuses? Again, I used these excuses to remain in my false contentment and to defeat myself. However, when we begin to see change as a method of growth, we allow many opportunities to arrive and welcome what may be successful or unsuccessful. For those who may need it, as I was one, let's change our definition of change. Here is how I break down the "change" of change:

- Introspective look
- Exo-spective look
- Self-realization of not living up to expectations
- Change as a negative
- Changing change from a negative to a positive
  - o Coin change builds up to dollars and riches.

- Change does not have to encompass bad qualities only.
- Even changing some good habits helps change the perspective on bad habits.

When I was in a state of depression, and not being a star, I would constantly question why. Why is no one calling me for the jobs I applied for? Why am I not meeting people? Why is my love life going down the drain? After that, I would answer, "Life just sucks!" Some may even have a more positive outlook and say, "It's the will of the world" or "My time will come." I said these things to reason why nothing was changing for me and everything was declining. As productive as I thought those questions were, they only fed into the state of emotion that I was spiraling into deeper and deeper. In fact, it sounded more like whining instead of doing.

Eventually, I realized I kept missing the important question, the one that scares us all: "What am I doing to CHANGE anything that is happening to me?" As I have mentioned before, this was the hardest step for me because it signified that everything bad that was happening, everything that was going wrong for me, and everything that I was not achieving was because of ME! At first, I was angry with the thought because it placed the BLAME on me. I did not believe I was perfect, but I knew I was good enough to do some of the things I pseudo applied myself to do. It also made me angry because if it were true, then it also shined light on my dependence upon the sympathy, empathy, and consideration of me from others and the universe around me. Funny thought, my ex-wife used to say I was dependent upon her. I always fought her about it. I would always say two married people should be able to depend upon each other, and if anything, our dependency upon each other was healthy. Even though I was right, she was right, too. She could never find a way to put it into words, but I depended upon her sympathy and consideration of me to the point where if I did not feel it was enough, I stifled myself and, in turn, stifled her. So, ex-wife, you were right!

Pinpointing the habits and personality traits that hold us back is a major challenge in itself. We are so geared to highlight the best in us that many times the worst in us becomes something to hide. Furthermore, many of us never seem wrong to ourselves. Either way, we are mentally wired to focus on the good in us so that it outweighs and overshadows our flaws. In all honesty, this leads to the biggest problem many people have with change: the feelings that accompany it.

Now the feelings that come along with the self-flaw discovery can range and seem overwhelming. For me, guilt and shame was built upon this discovery. It was so extreme that I even asked myself countless times, "How can I feel better when the medicine is making me feel worse?" Dealing with these feelings can become a struggle in itself, and it soon became a step to overcome for myself. It may seem a little backwards to break yourself down first, but with time and help from my life coach (yes even the coach needs some coaching sometimes), I was able to learn that these feelings resulted from my foundational perspective. I was living in a building (myself) that was dilapidated due to my foundation of blame, unworthiness and shame. I had to learn to change that foundation to one of responsibility, worth and growth. With this new foundation, I was able to build whatever I wanted. My building became anew due to this change in perspective. Instead of blaming others for my inabilities or negative experiences, I started to look inside to see how I could take control of my thoughts, habits and actions to create the changes I wanted. Instead of feeling unworthy about my non-accomplishments and ashamed of what little I had done in life, I began to take pride in what I have attained, where I am in life, and creating a plan based on my talents to grow in all areas of my life. So instead of being a repeat of the previous structure, the rebuild was newer, better and stronger. I created the growth I envisioned for myself.

Realizing that we must change ourselves is one of the hardest introspective looks we have to take. Some people are outright against change because it signals a lack or failure on their part, which can lead to that blameful, guilty, shameful feeling. However, we must take this introspective look and make honest assessments of it to be the stars of our lives. This begins the practice of maintaining a healthy self-perspective, one that remains honest and in the moment. Also, it helps us gauge an exo-perspective of ourselves. While it is true that we should not base our lives on anyone else's thoughts of how we should be, we should be mindful of our interactions with others and the perspectives they have through them. Using the insights of others is a healthy gauge to determine our overall personality and progress. When we are achieving goals and doing the right things, people notice our efforts, make comments about them, and want to be around us more often. So do not take outside thoughts of yourself lightly, but make sure you discern which are constructive and which are not. This can also be achieved with the help of a coach.

Can you recall your teenage years (or yesterday if you are a teenager reading this)? Do you remember waking up with that one pimple that was going to ruin your class picture? I am sure it sent your world into a chaotic frenzy that no one who called themselves your friend did not know about. Well, change is that pimple to many people; seeing themselves with such a blatant flaw just sends their world into a chaotic frenzy. But just like that pimple, with time and a plan, it will go away. It may have blemished this part of life, but life does go on. At some point, you will look back and realize how much you have matured and how well you can handle the same type of changes in the future.

I have learned a lifelong lesson, one that is going to enable me to not be afraid of being who I want to be anymore. It shows me that if I can free someone else, then I can free myself. I can picture myself reaching goals that I set for myself more frequently and efficiently. I find myself making my dreams reality and allowing myself to be heard with a true voice of who I am, instead of hiding behind someone safe and elusive. I find myself interacting with people more honestly and openly, being able to give them the freedom to share their thoughts and reciprocating the energy.

Now, you will experience the same. Let's hit the lights!

Lights

"And it wasn't until I placed the LIGHTS on MYSELF that I realized I needed to place the CAMERA and focus on MYSELF and then take the ACTION to better and progress MYSELF."

—*Me*

Have you ever heard the saying, "When life brandishes a great challenge, we find out who we really are"? The truth in this saying is 100% accurate. It is in those moments that we discover if our character is one of strength, determination and pursuance. Or we learn that we are lacking in desire, will and purpose, or that these things are not strong enough to motivate us. All it really takes is just one moment in our lives. In my moment of interpreting my dream, I realized that I was not showing the character or strength that I thought, no, that I knew I possessed. In that moment I realized that if any younger version of me saw myself, they would see a stranger or not be proud of who they had become. I realized that my life was a reflection of what my character revealed at that time. For me to change the reflection, I had to change what it reflected . . . and change myself. Inadvertently, I had stumbled onto the first step into my new role as the star of my life. It is the step I call "Lights".

Why is this step called lights? When I was running around believing life sucked, I was in the dark. I was looking for outside sources to show me who I was. I was blinded to the opportunities that my experiences were providing, not seeing any light of the day shine upon me. I call it lights because it is the process where we see ourselves for who we are right now at this moment. This is where we become naked in the light that shines on all of our blemishes and flaws. This is the light that we learn to shine to accent our best qualities.

Though this step sounds as simple as some self-reflection, it is as simple as some self-reflection. Sounds stupid, right? However, this is where it starts. All of our changes must start with ourselves, usually within ourselves. Many people try to make changes that reflect in their environment, people and habits, thinking that those are the only things that need to differ for betterment. However, self-reflection is the analysis of our own motivations, desires and needs. In the complete process, we must self-observe, self-criticize and self-discipline to change ourselves. Everything we do externally is a reflection of who we are internally. Self-reflection is taking the opportunity to remove all of the distractions, all of your environments, and all of the people around you. In doing so, you focus on yourself. In this step, we are making the self-observation and actually taking note of it, shining the light on how we truly are in the moment compared to the vision of ourselves to be.

It was difficult for me to experience that dream and then do some reflection. Let me clarify, the hard part was not having the dream, but realizing that it shined a light on who I was and how different I could be and the difference in making the choice to change my thoughts.

The hard part was coming to the realization that it was ME that sucked and not everything else around me. As much as we would like to believe, it is difficult for us to realize who we really are as individuals, especially in times of crisis or self-repair. How many times have you displayed a particular behavior notified, witnessed and proven by multiple people close to you, but you still deny it? Or how many times have you had a pretty good line to feed others to excuse your behavior, placing a Band-Aid over the wound but not treating it?

From where I am now, I look back on that moment and realize how trivial and minute the actual moment was. I am humbled by and appreciate how that moment was the hardest step for me to take. In fact, I appreciate how hard it is for anyone to make a self-realization that changes life in an awe-inspiring way. The process of making these self-observations is in no way a simple process. It is one that we must be humble and honest for, one that may kilter your world. It may even break your confidence. However, the thing to keep in mind is that a new confidence will build.

Remember that this is a process, and there are steps to take in this process. As with all steps, depending upon how you maneuver through each, you will find either a step up or a step down. Sometimes it is good to step up, and other times it is good to step down. Either way can be good as long as it pushes you closer to your goals. Let's get to stepping and shed some light!

Taking Light Steps for Mighty Leaps

The steps I am about to discuss are not chronological steps. They can be completed at any time, even throughout the Camera and Action phases of the process. In fact, they are needed beyond the process as a whole. Once you are able to use self-observation, self-reflection and self-discipline healthfully, you are able to become the alchemist of your life and what happens in it. These steps are more references to the honest and pertinent questions that we should be asking to gain a real and true perspective about ourselves.

When we shed this light, we shed the light in a couple of key areas. Our self-observation examines these key areas to gain a bigger picture of what is really going on with us. I have identified these key areas:

- Perceptions: Perceptions are how we generally view things. Perceptions are created with a multitude of factors, but the most important factor is what we think is good or bad for us.
- Habits: Habits are the routines and rituals that we follow. Some habits are those that we consciously make, while some may be of an unconscious nature.
- Catapults: Catapults are the physical, mental and habitual things in our lives that help us reach our goals and produce growth.
- Roadblocks: Roadblocks are the physical, mental and habitual things in our lives that deter us from our goals and negate growth.

When we take a moment to observe ourselves with a dedicated observational aspect, we find that we are looking at more than what superficially occurs in life. However, we want to start at the top and work our way to the root!

By deciphering the difference of "who we think we are" and "who we really are", we contrast observing superficially and observing with a dedicated depth. First, we must take a look at the "whats". We might ask ourselves: What do I want? What kind of car do I want to drive? What kind of home do I want to live in? What kind of people do I want to befriend? What job or position in life do I want? What is my salary? All of these are results we desire for ourselves and for others to see when we are observing "who we think we are". During this phase, we are looking at a result- and material-oriented model of ourselves, meaning we are looking at ourselves through the results of what is around and physically attained. These observations function as physical markers in our life that give us a "status" for ourselves so that others may see it, too. For example, if you make

$100,000 per year, live in a nice house, and have a wonderful family, then the superficial observation may be that you are in a great place in life because all seems to be in order, especially to those around you. Or what if you make less than $24,000 per year and you are unstably employed? The superficial observation may be that you are in a tough spot in life. Both are superficial observations, and each one can begin to put into perspective where you are in life, exposing "who we really are". Each example provides a great starting point in your observation, as it allows you to visualize a goal and make it concrete.

However, sometimes we find that "who we really are" does not coincide with "who we think we are" or "who we want to be". We may find that there is a particular level in life that we want to reach. If this is the case, then a new observation must take place. This observation must take a deeper and more specific look at not only the whats or results that are present now and desired but also the "whys". Because we already have the whats in mind or physically in front of us, the question then becomes "Why am I not who I think I am?" A dedicated observation exposes why certain things are the way they are and why they are not changing or changing in the wrong direction. This is also where we are able to observe different aspects in our lives, examining the weaknesses and strengths they offer to our desired self. You can break down your observations to your environment, to the people around you, or to available resources. No matter how you break them down, a dedicated observation always leads to what "you" are doing to promote or halt progress. Observing with a dedicated depth allows us to ask: What places am I in that either help or hinder this goal? Who am I around that either helps or hinders this goal? What habits and actions am I performing that either help or hinder this goal? By engaging in dedicated observation, we enable ourselves to make smaller, more manageable changes instead of such drastic, significant changes. By using a dedicated observation, you allow more opportunity for success in change.

Perceptions

One key to self-observation is perception. Perception involves two parts with each part being critical to the other. In fact, these perceptions drive a significant part of our lives, so they must be observed with an open mind and honesty. Ready? Here they are:

We all have a perception of ourselves that we would like to present to other people, and we value the perception that other people have of us. The perception we like to portray is one that springs from the mind but is desired to be materialized in reality. As much as all of us would like to deny it, we all care about what others think of us. We all may not be inclined to care what EVERYONE IN THE WORLD thinks of us, but EVERYONE IN THE WORLD does care what at least one person thinks of them. Even if you say, "I don't care what anyone thinks; I do my own thing", then you do care that others perceive you as independent, and maybe as a rebel. I call this external perception. Basically, external perception derives from the principles of social perception and visual perceptions. It is what we would like to see from ourselves and what we want others to see from us. It is important to take deeper observations of each because it places us in a reality of who we are. Here is why each is important to consider.

First, because it is simpler, let's explore the perception that others have of us. It is highly important that you keep in mind that this process is difficult. It is difficult because we want to put the perception we have of ourselves above others, which we should, but not for this part of the process. For this to be effective, we must learn how to take others' criticism as much as their praise, and try to be indifferent about each for proper evaluation. This is where you take an inventory of how people interact with you. If you find someone saying "why do you always . . .", it is time not to be defensive but to be open and ask "why do you see me this way?" You will not always be able to ask that specifically or even if you do, you may not get a direct answer; but with careful observation and guidance, you will be able to find your answers. Not too long from now, you will be able to use the views of others as a reference to who you see yourself becoming vs who you are not trying to be. You have already determined the results you desire from the inventory of others, so now you can determine how that inventory should change and what markers determine the progress. If a continuous inventory of those around you continue to produce the same results, then it can be assumed that you are either stagnant or moving toward someone you are not trying to be. But when you begin to see the difference in your inventory, and align it to the markers you have placed along your path, it becomes a visible and sometimes tangible sign of your progress.

Now we also have what I call internal perception. This is the perception of life based on how you are feeling emotionally. Emotions are the basis of the mental perception we hold of ourselves and our circumstances at this moment in our life. This mental perception is the general mood you give to life. Though your mental perception can be described through a multitude of emotions, there are only two generalities that our perceptions fall in, one being a negative-based perception. One example of a negative-based perception is the perception that "life sucks" and that everything around us is not making us happy. When going out into the world with this perception, the things we do are not fruitful and we seem to attract the wrong people for growth. Furthermore, it always seems like a hassle to go anywhere. The reason? When we start with a generally negative perception, we have already decided how we lose the battles and fail before we give ourselves a chance. I usually find this perception in people who do not have goals or visions. For some of those who do have a goal or vision, this perception can hinder them due to overthinking before the action is put into place. The generality becomes a catalyst for the actions and environment we partake in.

The other generality involves positive-based perceptions, where the mental perception is "life is grand". In this perception, everything we do, everyone we speak to, and everywhere we go has a positive light upon it because we view life as being a grand moment at this time. This allows for more opportunity, more growth, and more learning. It is the perception motivational memes attempt to inspire. As the negative perception becomes a catalyst for decline, positive perceptions become the catalyst for change and growth.

Now as perfectly normal humans, we are not perpetually in one generality over the other. We experience times where we view life in the negative, and other times in the positive. The goal is not to eliminate the negative perceptions completely but to construe them to make the perception generally positive. Also, we experience times when we may not be able to realize our general perception and may be stuck in one over the other. By periodically taking account of yourself, you can find which perception you are in. Sometimes it takes simple self-questioning and other checks include physical action. The simplest way to check your mental perception is to ask yourself, "How do I feel about life right now?" Take a look at the people you commune with and the places you frequent. How do those people and places make you feel? In answering these questions, we learn that our perception can have a significant impact on what life is perceived to be at this moment. For productive growth and change, this realization is one of the most critical aspects. It determines our moods, actions and interactions. I wish I had more to say here, but this step is really as simple as checking our mental perception by asking the right questions and performing actions to gauge the feeling they give us. Each perception shows where I am right now in this moment because I look at life as a journey; it must start with me and where I am right now.

Because I cannot go back and change my past destinations, I have to learn from them and forge a path to my decided and desired destination. With me being the starting point in this moment, it is best I begin with the heads up of positivity than the weight and drag of negativity. It also requires understanding that my decided destination is never going to be the end of my journey and therefore where I am right now must always be a positive start. Of course, bad things happen and bring us down at times. By staying focused on the destination, however, I can maintain a general head start in life.

Habits

> "Habits are the material manifestations of not what we want, but who we subconsciously are."
>
> —Me . . . again (and I'm sure a lot of other people)

Another part of shedding light upon who we are involves analyzing our habits. Not only can the reason why we have them hide in our subconscious mind, but the actual habit itself can sometimes become a subconscious blur to us as well. Many times we can have the desire to change our habits while being unable to because we do not know exactly what the habit entails. Even if we are aware of them, habits are some of the hardest things to break. So how does an effective change of your habits begin? It starts with identification. As the process continues, we will examine evaluation and action. For now, let's explore why it is important to observe and identify our habits. Of course, this is going to be a two parter: physical habits and mental habits.

Taking a deeper look at the habits we have in life provides a good reference to our internal and external perceptions. Many times our health, home, job and relationships are habits we create due to our perception, and then use to reinforce that perception. For example, I am a smoker. My external perception from others is mixed. Some want me to quit, my kids and past significant others. Some want to smoke with me. I met one of my best friends while smoking, and we still have a conversation over a smoke every once in a while. Others do not care what I do as long as it makes me happy. Based on this observation, my habit involves finding friends and girlfriends that either smoke or are okay with me being a smoker and not smoking around those that want me to quit. I determined that it was not a physical perception that kept me in a place of stagnation; therefore, there was no need to completely change it.

As for my mental habit and smoking, I had to observe other inner aspects and what I believed about smoking. As with the physical habit and external perception, my mental habit stems from and reinforces my mental habit. Analyzing when I smoked and why I smoked, I was able to define my internal perception: I generally like doing it. It does not affect my job, and personally it gives me a tool to relax. Furthermore, I have met some good people over a nice cigar or cigarette break. I am not worried about my health declining (even though the general public may be but that would not be my internal perception). I have a physical habit of working out regularly, and according to all of my doctor reports, I am still pretty fit for an aging man. I also do not have the mentality that it is something easy to quit. Generally, I just do not want to. The funny thing is, even though it is a habit, and I can smoke heavily at times, I can also go for extended periods without smoking . . . as long as there is an external restriction. I experienced a period in life where I actually stopped for two years due to a job assignment. Other times I have stopped for months due to other circumstances. So upon observing my habit of smoking, I decided that I would continue.

On the other hand, when I said I had to stop for two years due to a job assignment, the habit needed "complete change" and needed to be broken to reach a goal at that time. A long time ago, I experienced a situation in which I was just dismissed from college (because I am a realist I will admit I was kicked out), and I needed an avenue to leave my parents' house and find my way in the world. The quickest, easiest and most lucrative way appeared to be joining the military. I started visiting the recruitment office regularly to sign paperwork and to make sure my sign-up dates were on track. However, I still had one obstacle that hindered my entry into the military. I had a habit they did not allow: smoking marijuana. I had to quit smoking to pass the drug test to gain entry. Not only that, my recruiter told me they would perform random and periodic drug tests throughout my career, so I would have to stop smoking completely. Man, this was hard because I mentally and physically enjoyed the marijuana . . . a lot. I really wanted to leave my parents' house, so I had to make a plan to quit. As a result, the physical and mental roles had to change. Mentally, I had to prepare myself to make the changes I needed for the physical world. I had to observe when, where and with whom I smoked the most. Once I was able to determine these factors, I had to make routine changes to limit my exposure, my desire and my access. As a result, I worked more to use my time efficiently to prevent excess time for idle pleasures. I started associating with people who engaged in different activities, which allowed me to find new activities myself and to develop different trains of thought. It was not easy, though, as it generally took a couple of weeks to rid my system of what was present and to put a halt to the habit itself. Even though I have made it sound as simple as observe, plan and act, I asked my recruiter for four months to regroup before my entry date because I knew it would be a hard habit to break. Once identifying a habit and its cause, and the direction in which you would like it to change, it makes it much easier to create a physical, real change in habits.

Through these observations, I identified which habits were essential, which were benign, and which were more of a hindrance than anything else at the time. This is important as well, for we need to prioritize which habits need to be disposed of to make room for others, or which need to be prioritized more than the others. In identifying these habits, we are able to make physical changes that can make visible differences in our lives. The process of these observations, once worked, will make a world of a difference on your perspective and your capabilities.

Roadblocks and Catapults

The third part of shedding light is to shed light on the roadblocks that hinder us from change. This means observing our lives and seeing who, what or where we need to avoid if we desire progress or, as you guessed, the physical roadblocks. It also addresses mental roadblocks that may be preventing us from having a better perception and thus creating detrimental habits. These are the whys in life.

Observing our daily and routine lives in detail allows us to identify which of these are roadblocks, and which are catapults. Many methods exist to identify both roadblocks, but my personal recommendation is to hire a trained and licensed professional to guide you through these steps. I am not saying they cannot be done alone, however. For some that may be easy, but for others, if you are finding it difficult to determine your hindrance, then find some help!

Before we dive into a process that I believe can assist your life, I want to insert the disclaimer that this book cannot substitute hiring a trained professional. This book cannot be a substitute for a therapist or psychologist, or anyone who has clinical or medical training. This book offers a general process that can help you throughout periods in your life; however, the expertise of these individuals can help you specifically navigate certain periods of your life. Also, this book may offer great advice, but it does not substitute for a personal coach. As someone who has utilized the services of a personal coach, and being one myself, a coach is able to help you specifically deal with objections and assistants in your life. A coach is a great choice when you may not need medical or clinical assistance but may need some help with aspects you seem unable to control by yourself. Nevertheless, I will say that this book can be used as a tool between you and your professional of choice. It contains great insight that can help you uncover aspects of your life that may need more focus.

Roadblocks

With that being said, we can discuss why identifying roadblocks is healthy for your change. If we take the word roadblock and dissect it, it is road and block put together. Well, the road is your journey, right? And if it is blocked, then how are you supposed to get to where you want to go? As a coach, I have found many people who have gone through the process of observing their perceptions and habits, and even have made changes, only to backslide into who they previously were. Many times they will excuse themselves with statements such as "I'm just lazy," "It didn't work for me," or "this is too hard." In doing so, they allow themselves to fall back into a state of comfortable discomfort. I tend to find these individuals are not "lazy", nor that the process does not work, or that it is too hard. Many of these individuals have not been able to identify the roadblocks that keep them stagnant or even moving backwards. Honestly, this is the most important step to shedding light on who we are. For if we cannot remove the roadblocks, then how do we move anywhere?

Physical roadblocks are much easier to tackle than mental roadblocks, but removing them is still not an easy process. When identifying the physical roadblocks of our lives, we must look at the whos, whats or wheres in life that are not good. Usually, I would say that we need to look at both the good and the bad, but for this particular roadblock, the focus is mostly on the bad. We all carry bad baggage in the forms of people with whom we associate ourselves, places that we go, or even what we are currently doing. My example of this would be my career path. I had always thought of writing this book and becoming more of a coach. About ten years ago, I was nowhere near achieving those goals, which is the "what". Nor was I associating myself with the minds I wanted to imitate. With whom was I associating? The co-workers at my job, a bunch of nice guys and girls who were not nutritional to my growth in coaching. And the where? Well, I was not going to the classes, events or places I needed to go to experience growth. It did take me some time to realize that there were some roadblocks in my routine life. However, soon after, I learned that it was up to me to remove them.

It should also be noted that physical roadblocks tie heavily into physical perceptions as well as physical habits. This is why it is important to observe and identify these roadblocks. For example, let's say you want to be a swimmer, not just a pool swimmer, but one of those swimmers who jump into the ocean and swim continent to continent. Okay, there might be some exaggeration there. Let's just say you want to be a swimmer who is able to swim for long distances and over long periods of time. However, you also find that you are not near that goal. This is where we identify those physical roadblocks. First, let's start with where. To swim, you need water. How often do you visit a body of water? How do you plan on swimming or becoming an awesome swimmer if you are not in water regularly? Let's move on to the what. What are you doing to become a better swimmer? Are you taking lessons? Are you in the habit of swimming for at least an hour a day? Are you physically capable of being a good swimmer, and if not, what are you doing about it? Now on to the who. Are you networking with other swimmers? Coaches? Just answering these questions is not finding your roadblocks. If you are doing these activities with consistency, then you can assume you have little to no roadblocks. However, if you find that you are lacking in any of these areas, then the question now is why. In that answer you will find the roadblocks. Are you not in enough water because there is a drought or you live in a barren desert? That would be a "where" roadblock. Are you not practicing swimming because you keep losing your breath? Or do you find yourself a little obese to swim properly? That would be a "what" roadblock. Are you not around other swimmers because your circle of friends is more into badminton and you end up slapping some shuttlecock instead of swimming? That would be your "who" roadblock.

These are the observations that help mold the habits and perceptions you need to reach your goal. Start dressing in your swim shorts whenever you can, or when your friends come around. By placing yourself in the uniform of what you desire, you create a picture for yourself and those around you. This picture then becomes reality because there is now a physical act that accompanies your mindset. Through observation you will notice the difference between when you did not wear swim shorts and when you decided to do so regularly. Upon creating this picture repetitively, you create the observational perspective that you are serious about being a swimmer. This helps reinforce not only your belief of being a swimmer but also the belief of those around you. In turn, this reinforcement helps decimate the "what" roadblock.

As for that "where" roadblock, make a habit of going to a pool and swimming for an hour. By doing so, you are acting in your perception. Whether you practice or not, by placing yourself in the environment every day, you will find that your perception changes, making you more confident each time you go to the pool. Eventually, you will reach a point where you are getting in the water not only to splash around but also to practice your strokes. To start swimming longer. To start entering swim meets. Of course, this will happen after meeting some regular swimmers.

Once you start visiting the pool regularly, you meet a couple of swim enthusiasts and a coach or two. This satisfies your "who" roadblock. As you find people who have a like mind, you will find your interactions with them greater and more challenging (in a positive way). They can provide assistance in a plethora of ways, but mainly by giving you the power to remove the "who" roadblock.

Based on the previous examples, many of these roadblocks can be layered upon each other. By taking care of one, you may take care of many. It involves putting one foot ahead of the other, and the observation of putting one foot ahead of the other leads to great success. It may take time, but it does build and empower your actions throughout. This is how observing physical roadblocks can help you move to a better place.

Mental Roadblocks

Earlier in the physical roadblocks section, I told you to question why. Sometimes the "why" is not as simple as it being where, what and who. Sometimes it is something that is internally manifested. This overlaps heavily with mental perception as well as mental habits. As with your mental perception and mental habits, it is all mental. I would never say "it's just a mental thing" . . . but it is. If your perceptions are of an ill nature as well as your mental habits, then it most likely stems from a mental roadblock.

Let's go swimming again. At this point, your physical roadblocks have been identified. Now, you have a pool in front of you, a swimming coach to help you practice, and even a nutritionist who put you on the right plan to get you in swimming shape. However, you still cannot swim. The "why" might be because you are afraid of water. Therefore, the obvious question then becomes, "How can you become a swimmer if you are afraid of water?" Or maybe you are not a swimmer because of a disability to learn and everything your coach tells you seems difficult to comprehend. As a result, your three-week class becomes a three-year class overtime. This might indicate a mental roadblock.

The one thing about mental roadblocks that make them the most difficult to identify and even change is that many of them stem from emotional places. They can stem from trauma, a moment of joy, a moment of pain or sadness, an ego problem or, what I find mostly, fear. Because the mental roadblocks stem from emotional places, they become a part of us, ingrained and somewhat of a life philosophy.

Ever since I was young, my mother and father spent a significant amount of time apart due to my father's military career. Even though they were apart, they made it apparent how they worked as a team and as partners to ensure their household was stable and that we all were provided for. They always discussed their finances and made sure my sister and I knew what they were planning, even with discipline. My sister and I never had the luxury of going from one parent who said "no" to the other parent hoping they would say "yes" because we already knew they conferred and agreed on what my sister and I should be doing. As I grew older, I admired the partnership they had; it was something I desired in my own relationships. Fast forward to the future, my wife and I became a family. However, her upbringing differed from mine; therefore, her views significantly differed from mine. For the longest, we would try to work together, but it was something that we just could not do. We could never partner on our finances. Even though we agreed on a general way to raise our kids, we highly disagreed on how to discipline and navigate them through daily chores. We were both unaware of the root of the issue but agreed that WE were not working. It sent us both into a fit of depression and some seriously sub-par performance in our work, home life and all else. I, myself, would start many projects and look for her help with those projects only to be met with her non-interest. For the longest, I used that as an excuse to be sub-par. I used it as an excuse to justify why I was not landing the jobs I thought I should have had. In fact, I used her as an excuse so much that it turned into something vile and degrading. She became the ultimate reason why I wasn't shit, and without her being my "partner", I would never be shit. Totally unfair for both of us. I especially felt uneasy because even though I could not articulate what the roadblock was, I knew one was there. You see, my mental roadblock stemmed from a great example of a married couple. However, it became a roadblock because I felt as if I was not getting what I needed, which was being that great example of a married couple. As you can see, even bad roadblocks can stem from something positive.

It took me almost nine years to identify that roadblock, and I had to do it with many years of marriage and individual counseling. I also had a great coach alongside my counselor. They both helped me identify my strengths, weaknesses and opportunities, and they helped me devise a plan for my life that started with me. With that help, I learned that roadblock stopped me from being the successful person I knew I was supposed to be. And again, I had to identify that I was the roadblock in that situation. Therefore, I had to do the work to remove it. I will say this, though: once you can identify your mental roadblocks, this whole process becomes 100 times easier. As with all change, it starts with us, and how far ahead we put ourselves on the path along our journey.

Catapults

The one good thing about identifying roadblocks is that it also helps identify the catapults in our lives. Just like roadblocks, there are physical and mental catapults, each with the same stipulations of who, what, where and why. Unlike the roadblocks, catapults are the things that are in line to help us reach our destination. When identifying catapults, we identify the good to maximize the effect in the later process. Identifying these catapults is significant to change because it reinforces us to do the right things to get us where we want to be. And in change, we welcome and appreciate all of the positive reinforcement. The one thing about catapults is that regardless of whether they are physical or mental, they all help physical and mental perceptions and habits. Ready to take another plunge?

Here we are wanting to be that swimmer again. In going through your observation process, you find that you have been watching a plethora of instructional swimming videos. As a result, you decide to watch even more until you actually get to a pool. Even though you may not be able to get to a pool right away, you are in the physical habit of practicing techniques you have watched all throughout your workplace, air swimming through everyone's cubicle. Now you have catapulted your mental perception into saying, "This is something that I can do; in fact, I have been doing it." Once you get to that pool, your confidence catapults significantly, increasing your chances of becoming that swimmer. Giving yourself that mental and physical head start does wonders. Even when your coach tells you that you are doing something incorrectly, it is now easier to fix because you know the terminology and even some of the techniques. That is how you catapult into becoming that medal winning, news making, English Channel swimmer.

Identifying the catapults in your life will also be the best weapon you will have on your journey. These catapults will be your grace when you feel incapable. These catapults will keep you guided, on track, and continuously working toward your goals.

In the same example, when I identified the roadblock in my life, I also found that even though my wife and I were terrible partners, there were some things we had in place that would help me become a successful coach later in life. Okay, I am lying! There were none there. However, I was able to identify other areas in which I had catapults. I was experiencing some tough times and needed some sage advice and guidance from a professional. In those sessions, it was stated that I sought to be a coach and mentor for others. Well, that professional ultimately became a "who" catapult and gave me my first coaching assignment due to my "what" catapult, my ability to teach. You are reading this book because of the confidence instilled in me from those catapults.

The purpose of catapults is to launch us deeper into desired territory; therefore, they must be identified. Later, we will learn how to maximize the effects of these catapults to uncover not one but many.

Now that we have a brief understanding as to what shedding light does and where to shed that light, we are one step closer to achieving the goals we have and reaching the destination we desire. It is imperative that you also keep in mind this is an ongoing process, and one that can be used for just a general change or for a more directed change. In fact, you will find the more you practice these observations, the more direct the changes will be in your life. Again, observe your habits, roadblocks and catapults with an open mind. Observe them well and keep observing. You have dropped all of the distractions and replaced them with a focus. In other words, you have shed the background and ambient lights and created your spotlight. Time to break out the Camera!

Camera

Now that we have identified the perceptions, habits, roadblocks and catapults in focus, we must delve deeper into how to make them work for your progress . . . effectively. First, we all know how difficult it is to change someone's mind when they are dead set on believing something. Well, that "someone" is you now, and you have the task of changing your own mind or molding your perceptions. Also, how many people believe changing a habit is like making a new year resolution, something that is made in haste and not planned out and fizzles after the second attempt to go straight? Well, Happy New Year! Without the changing of habits, there can be no progress, so let's make it an awesome year this time. And, of course, you cannot forget about those roadblocks and catapults. Again, it is time for you to get your hard hat on and remove the roadblocks and put on your flight gear, for you have to use each catapult to fly higher than ever before. For these changes to be effective and long-lasting, we need to take time to make these changes an integral part of our lives. You must plan out how these changes will occur in your general life and then determine how to implement them into your daily or routine life. Lastly, you must implement the plan, but that will come in a later chapter. For now, let's focus on focus.

To address the focus of the perceptions, habits, roadblocks and catapults, we must deal with change. One aspect of change is the general perspective many of us have. When we typically think of change, it carries a negative connotation. Even something as simple as changing the batteries in the remote control, or changing a tire, has the implication that something went wrong and needs to be fixed. For many, this could be the roadblock. For me, it was one. What I came to realize was that my mental perception of change was wrong; therefore, my habits reflected me not wanting to change. I had to learn that change is just the rearranging of things not to fix but to make better. In reference to myself, I had to think of change as not a "fix" for my actions but a way to make more actions more rewarding. For example, if you were to take all of the change in your pocket to the bank at the end of every day, then change would be good, really good over time. In monetary terms, the adding up of change (even though it is small) can create huge sums. Each bit of change is a positive for me, and it makes my life balance higher. That is exactly the type of change we are doing to ourselves, maximizing our potential for the situations at hand.

This tool is a process to help you work through that change. The process is to ensure that change can be a lighted stairway up as opposed to being a dark, downhill road to nowhere. By utilizing the process, it will enable your change to have purpose and direction. Therefore, you will find your change emerging faster and more abundantly than you ever could imagine. It will assist you in focusing on your future through perceptions and habits and how to get there. Incorporating change into your life will help you conquer all obstacles. One of my inspirations is realizing that nothing changes until you change it!

There is a significant reason why I call this section "Camera". When using a camera, especially if it is not on a phone, some adjustments need to be made to make the shot work for the picture or the video. Sometimes it is the lighting or the flash setting. Other times it is the brightness or darkness. Or maybe it is the sharpness of the items in the frame. Adjusting all of these items creates a clear in-focus picture. It is only because of these adjustments that we are able to make the picture clear. The same adjustments, in-focus picture, and clear scene also apply to our lives when addressing change. In this case, you are the camera, the instrument used to focus and make the picture clear. Whenever we are not seeing ourselves "in-focus", we must make adjustments and changes to focus ourselves. This is where the adjustments are made to align and bring into clear focus your picture-perfect scene, life in the vision of who you want to be. Your scene is perfect because it entails all you need to overcome the trials and obstacles that enable you to pursue your vision. Through a camera, we always see the elements that create the scene before us. Usually, it is the setting, if there are any props, and any crew workers or cast members. It is the same with this camera, in which we focus on the props that enrich our lives. Placing the things you need to create who you want to be in the right arrangements will bring the scene together, allowing yourself to see how the smaller manipulations in a scene can change its whole perception on the viewer or actor. The same applies to life. Camera is the process in which you will find yourself putting your props into place to create the scene you have chosen for the set of your life.

Some of you might ask, "So, what does this focus mean? I thought that identifying and observing were enough." My answer to that is, for some it is enough. Those people have already put this book down and are moving to new heights. However, if you are still reading, or have only tried the observation stages and picked up this book again, then that should explain whether it is enough.

As for the definition of focus, let's dive into it. The camera part of the process addresses focus in certain areas, which includes self-evaluation and planning and strategizing. Each is significant to placing focus on what makes you, and each will have its advantages when moving on to the action part of the process. Let's explore those advantages.

Self-evaluation

Self-evaluation sounds pretty simple and self-explanatory, right? That is because it is. It is also important that we understand the difference between observation and evaluation. When you observed, it was strictly to identify aspects that could use changing or a boost. Evaluation is where you take those aspects and discover how they help or hinder you. This is where we dissect those aspects and get more detailed about the details. For example, to get from one part of a house to another, sometimes you have to pass through a cluttered room. Have you ever had to declutter a room that was filled to the brim with stuff? There might be a pile of old, tarnished, rusty trophies in the far left corner, all gathered from old accomplishments and deeds. A pile so high that you forgot you accomplished so much. In the far right corner rests a dust gathering magnet in the form of a pile of magazines and books. Wait, several piles. Each reaching to the ceiling and covering nearly half of the room. Let's not forget the disarray of clothing, strewn in piles and over piles of other things. Boxes of old videos, and toys, and just an extreme, utter mess. To create a path that allows forward progression, you walk into the room and realize that to get to the other side you must clear this mess. That is the observation in this process. Now that you know what needs to be done, it is time to plan and strategize how you will do the work to be quick or efficient. You must determine if all of those books and magazines are trash or if they hold information worth keeping to help you do what needs to be done in the other room. You must determine if those trophies are worthy of being kept. Do they promote a version of you that is long gone, or can they be polished and shined, and perhaps give you more motivation to keep clearing to move on to the next room? Let's not forget about determining if any of the clothing should be used or sold. For instance, if the other room is a kitchen, and you find an apron in those piles, then maybe it might be beneficial after all. Then after that, you must create a system to utilize and organize what you are keeping. You might have to determine how to get rid of the stuff deemed not worthy as well. The main goal is to get to the other room, so you ask yourself does this stuff has to be sold or trashed now, or can you just move it to the side for now, and once in the other room, devise a plan for the yard sale. This is the evaluation process. You are decluttering your life to make room for the things that are needed. You are also determining what is needed to make that room (your life) livable and usable.

Now that those concepts have been clarified, let's talk more about self-evaluation and how it is used to progress you. First and foremost, you must have an open mind and be honest with yourself about who you are. Next, you must be honest about who you would like to be, and where your journey will take you, for this now becomes the desired result. I am sure you already have some idea of who the desired you is, as that is why you picked up this book in the first place. With that in mind, we are able to take microscopic looks. When you perform your evaluation, you want to ask yourself these questions:

Which perceptions/habits are real and which are only envisioned?

This is the first important question to ask because this is where we determine the real perception we gather from external sources, but more importantly, we determine who we really are vs. the image we have created in our minds. Now there is nothing wrong with having a vision of who you want to be, but it does not help if that vision is not reflected in our lives. Therefore, going through this step creates a foundation for us to build upon. Sometimes that foundation is close to where we want to be, and sometimes that foundation is far off from what we desire. When I started this process, I just knew I was the life of any party. I knew that everyone enjoyed my company and I was always wanted everywhere by everyone. I know, this is extremely vain. Sometimes I can be. After going through this process, however, I found that the vision I had was not one of reality, and it was not because people did not like me or that my company was not appreciated. The truth is, I hardly talked to anyone, hardly went anywhere and hardly did anything. I was not the people person that I thought I was. In reality, I was living the life of a hermit. However, I knew that I desired to interact with people, and I wanted to be that vision I had of myself. Therefore, it was a reality check once I learned that my foundation was completely different from what I envisioned. Nevertheless, it still gave me a place from which to start and build. I am still working on this aspect, but I am attending more social events: seminars, workshops, and even one of my newly found favorite activities, glassblowing classes. I am making efforts to speak to new people and make more friends and connections more often. Meeting people that share my interests at these seminars, workshops and glassblowing classes gives me a wide range of networking, mentoring and companionship to enrich my life and my goals. This has also enabled my efforts to speak to my friends more often, thus creating a circle of "social interaction", the thing I knew I desired. I am making efforts to speak to more friends more often as well. With this self-evaluation, I was able to determine what was real vs what was not.

What is the extremity of change needed to change the real to the envisioned?

Once I was able to determine what was real and what was not, I then had the necessary tools to determine how extreme of a change I needed to make to get to the person that I had envisioned myself to be. In this particular example, I noticed that my range of change was pretty extreme. I know and understand first-hand how this can be disheartening or discouraging. If that is the initial feeling, then remember that this is still a tool. It is a tool to determine how much time and how much work you must invest into the change. Given this advantage, we can actually look at any extremity with more confidence and understand that no matter how extreme the change has to be, it can be done with time and work. Determining the extremity of change also gives us a clearer perception of who we are vs our envisioned self. Therefore, it adds and reinforces the foundation that has already begun when determining what is real vs what is not.

How do I implement more of the envisioned perception/habits while breaking down the real?

I myself find this one of the most exciting steps of the process. As you go through the process, you will find that many of these steps overlap into others. This evaluation overlaps into many steps. If determining what is real vs what is not and the extremity of change were side dishes, then this part of the evaluation would be your steak. This is the part of the evaluation in which you determine what steps are needed to make broader and efficient changes. I find this part exciting because I label this the step of "great expectations". It is where we set the expectations of the changes we need to make. We set the expectations of what such change will do to our lives. We set the expectations of how this affects our interactions with people. We set the expectations of what needs to be done to reach our destination of our envisioned selves. It is also where we set the expectations of how to dissolve the perceptions and habits that are not helping us. This is where we set the expectations of who we want to be. This is where that vision of who you want to be starts to become a reality. Great expectations are real and necessary for us to reach certain levels in life. This is the step where visible changes begin to occur, changes that we make in ourselves, especially in the mental aspects of this process. It is where we can pinpoint and determine the action needed to part with certain perceptions and habits, which is an exciting change in itself. I also find this step exciting because it forces you to set the expectations of what your life is to be. For there is no need to be on this journey if you do not have a destination in mind. Once we have that expectation and destination, it then becomes a goal, a goal to be reached and attained. It follows suit with the other expectations as well.

Therefore, I hope you find this step as exciting as I found it to be.

As for the roadblocks, this line of questioning is something that we must be honest with again. I know some people are able to follow this book with ease and no external help, but for those who are not as adaptable, I urge you to find professional assistance, especially for mental roadblocks. With that said, the questions that help evaluate those roadblocks are questions that answer how they impact your progress. So here we go!

Which roadblocks are hindering me?

If it has not been done already, then please identify your roadblocks. This is the first step in being able to evaluate the hindrance on your life. Again, these roadblocks can be physical or mental, but still a blockage either way. Once identified, a real evaluation can begin in determining if those roadblocks are hindrances to your specific goals and destination. Some roadblocks may not even play a factor in what we need to change. This step is to help you determine which are ripe for change and which are not. For example, even though it would be helpful to get over your fear of water, it does not impact your ability to fly a plane. So even though it is a roadblock, it may not be one that must be addressed at this time. Nevertheless, having a fear of public speaking will have an impact on you if you plan on becoming the next motivational guru. Yes, I am talking about me here. I have a fear of deep, natural bodies of water, but I have flown a plane. And yes, I do have a fear of public speaking, but I hope to be your motivational guru. So take this time to determine which of those identified roadblocks are hindering you from your goal and focus specifically on those.

How are those roadblocks hindering me from my envisioned self?

Once you determine which roadblocks are a hindrance, you can explore how they are hindering you. To do so, you must compare your envisioned self to your current self and determine exactly what that roadblock does to keep you from being that envisioned person.

For instance, my fear of public speaking will hinder me from being a motivational guru because I have to speak in public to large groups of people. By making this comparison between your two selves, it helps to make obvious how the roadblock is a hindrance.

What can I do to remove those roadblocks or to change them into catapults?

By seeing how each roadblock is a hindrance to us, we can determine how to remove the blocks or change them into catapults. This step allows us to take those roadblocks and examine how we reinforce them in our daily lives. By being able to determine how they affect our lives, we can then determine how to change them. Some roadblocks might require a single action, while others might require a whole other process to get through. But this step is where that is determined. Here we can create the process needed to change those roadblocks. For instance, to get through my roadblock of public speaking, I had to do more public speaking. I also realized that my fear of speaking also kept me from speaking my mind in other places where my opinion or knowledge would have been welcomed. So I had to speak more, not just in public, though. I had to utilize every opportunity that I had to speak. And even now, even though I may speak in large groups or for larger crowds, I *still* am working through this roadblock. With each speaking engagement or opportunity, I am removing more and more of that roadblock. I even consider it a change to a catapult. As with every opportunity, I become better at my craft and find that each opportunity is more rewarding than being quiet and afraid, or being stuck as who I was instead of who I am. I also want to point out that the consistent thing about breaking down the roadblock is action. I know we are not at that chapter yet, but please take important note that if no action is taken, then you are basically stuck in being quiet and afraid. This is regardless of the amount of observation, planning and strategy. For any hindrance to be removed, or blockage to be cleared, it requires some work and action. If I had not acted on my roadblocks, then I would not be who I am today, and you possibly could not have been reading this book. That is the importance of action to your change. We will discuss more on action later.

Just because something remains a roadblock does not mean you cannot find a way to work through it, or that you can continue to use it as an excuse to remain stagnant. If we allow them to keep us still or digressing, then those roadblocks begin controlling us instead of us controlling them. Sometimes a roadblock can happen in momentous occasions, forcing us to make split second decisions. Others can be ongoing and stasis, creating longing anxiety or fears. Sometimes the roadblock can be a mental aspect, us holding ourselves back because of the way we think about something. And other times it can be a physical roadblock, like living in a city far from your desired dream job. Everyone experiences their roadblocks differently and must handle them according to what is best for themselves.

For instance, I know I did not like deep water but I swam frequently throughout my life and I even took training to save lives privately and in my military career. All of these efforts helped me physically prepare for such moments. However, I also would mentally place myself in different scenarios where I found myself in deep water. In each scenario, I would take mental notes and shadow how I would escape the situation, mentally preparing my actions for whenever the scenario would become a reality. Now follow me here because this is a key pivot to my preparedness. In addition to mentally succeeding in escaping those situations, I also had to mentally place myself in the scenario that I had failed to escape those situations safely. I had to feel both sides of the coin. This allowed me to realize that the situation is going to end one way or the other in reality but preparation is still key. By doing this often, it allowed me to be more prepared and less fearful of the roadblock itself when it did arrive. It was the mental repetition and mental reinforcement of what I could do. For that particular example, my ex-wife says that once we spotted my daughter so far out into the water, she froze and it seemed as if I immediately jumped into action. What seemed like immediateness for her was all of that preparation throwing me into action, even before I could finish thinking about my fear of deep water and the results that this roadblock could create at that moment. Mental preparation and repetition were the best tools that I could have used. I cannot say that placing yourself in a scenario that causes you anxiety, fear, or any extremity of emotion is a healthy idea for everyone, so I am not recommending that. However, being prepared for roadblocks should be achieved to work through them. Everyone must prepare for such scenarios in a way that they find healthy for them. Sometimes this occurs through professional services, or sometimes simply by placing yourself in the scenario mentally. If you find a way to be prepared, then you will find that your roadblock will have less and less control over you. In all fairness, my children are grown now. However, my daughter knows that if we are ever at the beach, there is no amount of distance that she could put between us that I will not shorten to get her!

In my previous example, I had to face a roadblock instantaneously, which mostly came to mind at the same time my flight or fight and gut instinct kicked in. It was what the moment called for at the time. Though it was something I was prepared for, I still experienced a moment of loss of control and stagnation. Just a moment, though. However, I could have remained stagnant for that time, and my daughter could have drifted away to become a mermaid and live with the mer-people. There is not one thing I can say that will provide a breakthrough effect for everyone, as each person handles their roadblocks differently. But I can let you in on how I handled that roadblock as well as some of my current roadblocks. Because I am aware of my roadblocks, I intentionally place myself in a scenario mentally so that I can see how the situation or scenario makes me feel. Does it make me feel scared? Does it make me feel angry? As for this example, deep water terrifies me because of what lives underneath and water being a powerfully elusive force. Depending upon how the situation makes me feel, I then prepare for the moments I may meet along the roadblock.

Now let's address the catapults. As many of these have been identified as well, it is important to nurture, use and maximize your catapults. Your catapults are the things that give you an upper hand in the changes you want to make to become your envisioned self. The other benefit of catapults is that you have the ability to create them to suit your goals. In fact, it should be expected to create more and more catapults in your life to launch you deeper into your envisioned self. So with the following questions, we can evaluate how each catapult is helping us get closer to our goals.

Which perceptions/habits are catapults or potential catapults?

Once observed and identified, we can determine which perceptions and habits are catapults or have the potential to be. Plain and simple enough, right? Actually, this might be one of the simpler steps that we take along our journey. This is where we lay out each perception or habit we already possess and determine which one can catapult us into greatness. In laying all of our catapults out, we can form a general idea of what we are doing right. This is a broad view of our goodness, which gives us a good sense of confidence and usually the reality that we are much closer to our goals than we could have imagined.

If utilized, how will these catapults help me progress?

Even though this might sound like redundancy from the previous step, I assure you that it is not. In the previous step, we identified and evaluated our catapults to determine which are instrumental in reaching certain goals. This is where we match our catapults to our goals and determine which are pertinent for each other, where we take that broad perspective and make it more specific. We are able to determine how much of a boost each catapult brings, and to envision what each brings to the foundation we have set for ourselves. By making more detailed evaluations, we can attribute each catapult to a specific goal and area of our lives. So let's take my example of my fear of deep natural bodies of water. If my goal were to be that swimmer that swims the English Channel, then my catapults would be that I am an excellent swimmer and I have experience and training in bodies of water similar to the Channel. These catapults put me closer to attaining that goal of swimming the Channel. Just like with the roadblocks, some catapults will help us get to our desired goals, while others just won't. Again, all of the catapults that will help me become a great swimmer will not help catapult me into my goals of becoming a motivational guru. Thus, it is important to evaluate your catapults so that you are utilizing and maximizing the correct catapults for your specific changes.

How do I maximize the effects of my catapults?

Ahh, what a question to be asked. The answer is, you are already doing so. By taking the time to observe and evaluate your catapults, you have already given a major boost to those catapults. By categorizing which catapults are integral for each of your goals, that boost becomes even greater. As always, you can get even more potential out of each catapult. The key to getting that potential is to remember "more, more, more". If your catapult is an action, then do more of that action. If your catapult is knowledge, then gain more knowledge or teach someone your skills. If your catapult is a where, then be in that place more often. And so on. By continuing to practice these steps, you will find that all of their aspects evolve, including your catapults. Your catapults evolve into being productive tools that help you achieve your goals with more efficiency as well as achieve more goals overall.

How do I create even more catapults in life?

Well, by creating them. As mentioned before, once you are engaged with the process, you will see your catapults evolve as your goals do. This is one form of creating new catapults in life. With this method of creation, you will find that the catapults that you already have must meet the requirements of your goals. Therefore, every tweak and modification to your old catapults essentially creates new catapults. The other method is to examine your goals and to determine what you need to achieve them. By creating the scenario you envision, you also envision how to get there. In this envisioning, you must lay out the things that will help you reach that vision. Through this process you will be able to find, utilize and maximize new catapults. So if your ambition is to be swimmer, then decide how good you want to be, what is needed to achieve it, and how what you have or know already aligns with this goal. In doing so, you will find that you have catapults that you never knew existed. Therefore, you now have an extra advantage, which is always a great thing.

At this stage, we can see how the Lights process and observation and shedding light move us along the path of Camera and the evaluation of these observations. By performing these steps of the process, we have a firm foundation on what we know is real and not real about ourselves. We also have a foundation of knowing that we create the perceptions we have of ourselves as well as the perceptions others have of us. In turn, these steps give us the tools that we need within ourselves to create the reality of our envisioned goal. With this foundation and these building tools, let's draw up the plans for utilizing each. In the next phase of Camera, the planning and strategy stage, the whole vision will be drawn up into the blueprint of your life.

Planning and Strategizing

For this section, I plan to keep it short, but I do want to iterate the importance of this step, and the impact it will have on your life. To begin, let's recap an important detail in the evaluation stage. You have now created not just a vision but a goal! While some of us are great at setting goals and achieving them, some of us need more direction. Hell, some of us did not even know we should have a plan for our goals, as we just set them and simply hoped we would reach them by drifting through life or maybe even by magic. You and I both know change does not happen by magic, but it would be so much easier if it did. For those of us that do need help, this step will guide us through the process. To reach a clear and concrete goal, we must set a pathway to it. In setting that path, we decipher what helps us achieve progress and what achieves setbacks. We also go out and get the things we need to make that progress. Sound a little familiar? It should. You just went through pretty much a whole book saying the same thing, just in a different way. And to add, the reason I am keeping this short is because there are so many ways to plan and strategize your goal achievement that I could not list them all here. There are charts and tables that you can use as well as lists and notes. If you need assistance in finding methods, inquire with a trained professional or a life coach. Everyone uses a different method of strategy and planning, and the key is to find which method is most progressive for you. So now that we have the foundation of who we are, we decide how to build on it, where to build on it, the time in which it needs to be built, and how high to build it.

Action

Nothing Changes If You Change Nothing

Finally, we get to the good part, to the part we all have been waiting for. Throughout the book, I have mentioned taking action and the different ways you can do so. I have mentioned how your observations and planning are obsolete unless action is taken. I have also mentioned how your observation and planning involve taking action. Let's do a quick recap! You set the Lights and observed by examining yourself and uncovering the perceptions, habits and roadblocks that kept you stagnant and the catapults that gave you a boost. From there, you became the Camera. You were able to lay a good foundation to build focus and a clearer picture of your life. Then by modifying your old perceptions, habits, roadblocks and catapults, you were able to create new perceptions, habits and catapults, as well as a plan to tackle any roadblocks that would appear. These changes provided a blueprint for you to focus on as you figured out the necessary steps to reach your goals and how to implement them in your life. You did that, and that is taking what? See, you already know what comes next: Lights, Camera, and Action! Out of everything that has been discussed in this book, nothing will be more fun, rewarding and progressive than the "Action". The energy of want, will and determination create action, which is the movement toward reaching new goals. Just like the other aspects of change, action takes some work as well.

Now that you have done all of that observation and planning, it would likely be a shame if you did not act. For all of the parables, idioms and sayings spoken about the power of action, I think my favorite one is, "If you do nothing, then nothing is done." Besides, the guy who said it is awesome: me, of course. I say this because I know some people will observe and plan away, but when it comes time to put the plan into action, many factors will stop them from doing so. How do I know? Well, it's me again. I am some people! So how do we encounter that? As with all of these aspects of change, there are some general steps we all can take.

Thinking and Planning Are Different from Action

Before I started my journey, and even in the beginning of it, I believed that as long as I planned something out, or at least wrote my thoughts down, I was being active. It felt as if I was doing something, and I literally was doing something, so how could I see a difference? Many people do not even compare thinking and planning to action because they believe it is the same thing. I am afraid not, and here is how I learned that lesson.

At the risk of being contradictory, I must say thinking and planning is a form of action, but is it the action that will get us what we desire. It takes more than just thinking of a great invention to make a great invention. That is what we are doing here: re-inventing ourselves. The observation only gives us insight, while the planning only gives us direction. I was one that thought if the idea was good enough, then action would immediately follow. Maybe not my action, but the action of others, or just the universe enacting its will upon my superb ideas.

However, just having those ideas never surfaced in any of my plans or actions. It is not enough for the English Channel swimmer to observe and plan; he/she must practice and practice until the goal is done. That is the action. We also must remember that action does not have to be the biggest thing in the world. In fact, we will find that small actions often make huge impacts.

So if thinking and planning are not action, then what is action? In this sense, action is the movement that revolves around certain goals. I like to relate it to a revolution. In fact, if action is done correctly and efficiently in this manner, then it does lead to a revolution: one in your life and one in the prospects of a greater future. Like the revolution of our planet around the sun, one revolution ends at the beginning of a new revolution. In short, your action will provide opportunity and pathways for more action. It becomes a healthy and manageable cycle, if you are aware of what actions need be taken. For anything to happen, we must be focused on the action of doing it. For ages, I have had material to put into this book, and even thought about writing it years before I actually did. All of that thinking and planning did not produce the book, but it did influence me to write, which is the action that lead to you reading this book right now. Now that you are reading this book, I am able to offer speaking engagements and personal coaching on a bigger and better level. So, in turn, that action led to more action.

Analyzation and Accountability

Ready for our AA meeting? You know, analyze and accountability. Having taken the steps to create goals, and defined the actions needed to achieve them, we must analyze and account for those actions. It is not directive if we perform actions that are not important to our goals; therefore, many actions must be analyzed to determine if they are pertinent to our goals. For example, our swimmer has been practicing a lot lately, doing doggy paddles, and decides to act on their goal and attempt their first swim. The swimmer then learns it takes them longer than expected to reach a certain point. So now the swimmer must analyze their efforts with the doggy paddle. After careful analysis, and with existing information through observation, the swimmer decides to change his/her practices to a new style: the breaststroke. With careful planning, the swimmer incorporates this new style into practice. He/she then returns to attempting his/her goal of swimming the Channel. This time, the swimmer notices exponential progress with this new style, and renders the practicing of the other style as not a priority. Therefore, the swimmer witnesses more and more improvement bringing them closer to his/her goal due to the analysis of action.

Many people will engage in actions and not even verify if they are the correct actions to reach their destination. This is wasted energy, which is another drag on our psyche that can result in inaction. Analyzation is important because it gives us a clearer picture of our path and determines if it is the one we envisioned for ourselves. It also allows us to improve performance in three ways. First, analyzation provides great motivation to continue on our journey. Once we start seeing the progress we have made, we view accomplishments in small measures, which, in turn, can assist in the continuance of practice. For instance, we all want to continue a diet when we notice we have lost two, then six, then ten pounds. This also happens when we notice digression in our actions. With analyzation we begin to understand which actions not to take in the future, and which ones need to be taken henceforth. Our swimmer experienced this scenario when he/she learned the dog paddle was not as effective as planned. However, the analysis motivated him/her to continue to try to reach the goal. With that motivation, the swimmer was able to continue performing actions knowing a measurable amount of effort went into their progress. This instilled the motivation to keep moving forward. Even in the face of what seemed like digression, the swimmer decided not to forego the goal but to change the strategy because there was action put forth, which leads to the second importance of good analysis.

While a good analysis can help motivate, it also helps grade the strategy. Analyzation provides a good breakdown of how our actions are helping us reach our goals. It allows us to see which actions are efficient and effective at the same time. This step must be preceded by setting measurable achievements, in which you can compare your progress to your strategy. Once these measurements are set, you are able to grade your actions against the strategy you have envisioned. We are able to determine whether the actions we are performing are producing the right effects for the strategy we devised. Through analysis we find that the actions we have planned are pushing us closer and closer to those goals we aspire for, or moving us further away from them. With a deep analyzation, we can determine if the actions we are taking are fruitful toward our goals, or if they are feeding into different desires. For our swimmer, he/she had a measurable goal to achieve. By using that measurement, the swimmer was able to determine which actions were and were not efficient. As our swimmer continued to practice, he/she found the particular strategy he/she decided upon was not efficient. Therefore, through analysis, they then changed the strategy and found it to be more effective. It is through this analysis that we uncover whether we need further observation and planning, or if our plans and strategies require any changes.

Lastly, the ultimate importance of analysis of action is its ability to provide an incentive to stay motivated in addition to a strategy check. It also provides accountability for actions or non-actions already taken. This accountability is simply that you are performing action, regardless of whether it is efficient or not. It is ensuring we did what we were supposed to do. With many people, simply performing an action can be difficult. With analysis, we can say with pride that we did something, we are learning from it, and we understand how it affects any further action. Our swimmer made sure he/she practiced the different swim strokes, in turn, creating more measurable actions, creating more achievement and creating a cycle of action. Without the analysis, you cannot have accountability.

Of course, everyone has their own way of analyzing activity, and that is fine, as long as you are giving your actions an honest analyzation compared to what you desire. Along with analyzing your actions, however, you MUST HAVE ACCOUNTABILITY. As previously mentioned, accountability is making sure you do what you say you are going to do. Accountability can be kept in many ways, and as always, I implore that if you are not progressing with this step on your own, then seek some professional assistance. Accountability coaches offer great programs, so please explore them. It is important to maintain accountability as it keeps us on track. It keeps us aligned with our goals and focused on our aspirations. Accountability also shows us our progress and creates confidence in what we are doing. Even if what we are doing is wrong, accountability gives us confidence in knowing what needs to be changed and how. Accountability also gives us responsibility for our actions. In having responsibility for our actions, we then feel as though we are not just drifting through life, and it gives us clarity on the situation and what to do when life throws us curveballs. Therefore, we find less anxiety and more determination in the process of accountability. And again, there is nothing wrong with someone holding your hand during this process. In fact, it is one of those situations where you can build great relationships with those that are assisting or maybe even going through similar situations for similar goals. Another great thing about it is that when you do the right thing, you can be held accountable for that as well . . . and that is always a great thing to be accountable for.

Hopefully, by reading this book, you will have learned there are a number of ways to find help with accountability, more importantly, finding out enough about yourself to know which methods would be most effective. I know I mentioned it briefly before, but I want to make sure you know how adamant I am about each of these viable options. Because I am not clinically trained, I will always advise you to seek a therapist or a clinically trained counselor to help maintain accountability. They both have the advantage because either can be a medically or clinically trained individual that can give you great insight into how you view and interact with yourself. In addition, they are trained to detect conditions that could be physiological, which other professionals may not be able to detect. Through this practice of insight, the therapist or counselor can help advise and clarify some of your catapults and roadblocks and even uncover their root cause. In life, a therapist or counselor is always good to have just for the provision of insight about your progressive or digressive behaviors.

Some people may not need someone as in-depth as a therapist or a counselor but still may need someone capable of observing and communicating insight. In this instance, a coach is a great person to assist you through life and with accountability. A great coach enables you to express what you see about yourself and helps formulate a different perspective in the manner you desire. A good coach is also able to help a client navigate through roadblocks with advice and a plan to assist the client in self-correction. When you have a goal, and your coach helping you with a plan, with him or her being aware of your desired results, your coach can identify any impedance along the way. Most coaches will also hold you accountable for the actions needed to pass through the roadblock stage. This accountability helps ensure the work you do is about progression and is not done in vain, or done to result in digression. Having a great accountability partner functions as another way "to hold onto your guns". If you are aware and able to devise your own plan of action, and have the discipline and will to stick with it, then you are awesome. However, some of us do not have this ability but may not need the full professional service menu for assistance through periods of growth. Some people may need someone more like a partner, who may have similar roadblocks or goals, and they are able to keep account for each other. A great accountability partner will be one that ensures you are focused on the goal and will be there to motivate you in the time of roadblocks. In turn, you would provide the same motivation to them in their times of need. Being accountable to someone else also enforces accountability to ourselves, as it enables the mentality of having to do what needs to be done. By having a great partner, you will find that less motivation from each other is needed over time and the accountability becomes to one's self. Nevertheless, we are still going to be proud to show others the accomplishment and still cherish the bond shared through this accountability of each other. There is also the possibility of being your own accountability coach and partner. A sense of pleasure and pride exists in knowing you can set a goal, put forth a plan, and complete the actions needed without the help of anyone else. Any way you decide to keep your accountability, ensure that it is right for you, and that it is measurable and part of a plan toward reaching your goals.

In reviewing this step, we begin to understand how action not only plays a vital role in achieving goals but also is vital to anything we want to achieve. As long as your actions include an honest analysis and you have accountability, then your actions will be rewarded with progress toward your goals.

Post-production

When you combine the Lights, the Camera and the Action, you create a production. Relating it to life, we find that your "ultimate vision" is the production, while each step you previously took made the production possible. As in film, when all of the lights and cameras are put away, and the actors have played their parts, the post-production follows. This is the step in film where constant editing is done to ensure all of the frames fit. Any voice or sounds that need to be added are done here, even the special effects and all of the things that continue behind the scenes. The same thing applies when your life is the set. You have gone through the observations and created a strategy to pursue your goals. You have put forth action, and now you are on your way. It is here that the post-production occurs. It is where you continue the process until you achieve the results you desire. This is where you understand your observations never stop and continue to evolve and change around you. This is where you implement the analysis of your strategy. You are able to decide if the steps you are taking are on the correct path. If they are not, then which way to go is less of a question and more of a choice for you to decide.

And, of course, you realize that it all takes vigilant action, the action being a reflection of all of these processes used together as a tool. Being in the post-production stage of life involves all three stages of Lights, Camera, and Action, as it is a progressive movement toward your goals in life. If your goal is fortunate enough to be reached through the process, then there is one other action many people do not take the time to do, and I believe it is the biggest disservice to your work and progress. Many people fail to take pride in their accomplishments, missing opportunities to show others what they have achieved and to help them achieve their goals as well. This serves as a benefit in your life because I am a firm believer that to fully learn something, you must teach it to someone else. There is no use in making a film if no one is to see it, talk about it or want to live it. So be that film, live that film and be proud of the production you have created!

Conclusion

As we have learned, life does not have to suck because life is what we make it. We are able to make it what we want. Upon reviewing the full process, we also found that we have the power to do so, as long as we have the will and the plan. And speaking of the plan, do not forget that this is a continuous process, not only for one goal or aspect of life but also for the entire wheel of your life. By shedding light you create your own spotlight. Lights! Instilling observation into your life and taking the time to better yourself by learning yourself. Learning the perceptions that you carry and the habits they create. Exposing the roadblocks that burden you to transform them into catapults that help you soar to your goals. You learned that a continuous practice of this process will always give you building blocks and tools to expand upon and grow. Then by becoming your tool of change, the Camera, you created your perfect scene, devised the props and scenery needed, and focused on the masterpiece you envisioned.

You uncovered the relations between your life perception and your choices and how they create the scene you live in. You discovered ways to master your set of life, and placed important people, places and things along your path to a better you. Lastly, you learned how action is a direct reflection of your perceptions and a pathway to being a grander you. You learned that to do things, you must do things. You learned that it may be hard, but with a purpose and a path, it is achievable. And it all becomes even easier the more you put the plan into action.

I hope you have found this book helpful to your journey. I also hope that whenever you need a little motivation in your life, you are able to pick up this book and receive the positive reinforcement you need. Even if you are not in a bad position, but need some help reaching your goal, then pick up this book and go through the process again. Use it to your advantage so that it can become a necessary tool for your greatness. Turn on the Lights, the Camera, and the Action!

And there have it . . . YOU are now the STAR of your Life.